# 哈啦陽光山丘

三民書局

Snooze and Snore    ISBN 1 85854 663 X

Written by Gill Davies and illustrated by Eric Kincaid

First published in 1998

Under the title Snooze and Snore

by Brimax Books Limited

4/5 Studlands Park Ind. Estate,

Newmarket, Suffolk, CB8 7AU

# 努努和諾諾
## Snooze and Snore

*twin* [twɪn]
形 雙胞胎的

*mice* [maɪs]
名 老鼠（複數）

*moss* [mɔs]
名 苔蘚

*hollow* [`halo]
名 洞，穴

Snooze and Snore are **twin mice**. They live in **Moss Hollow** on Sunshine Hill.

嗒嗒和諾諾是一對雙胞胎老鼠。他們住在陽光山丘一個周圍滿是青苔的洞裡頭。

*rascal*
[`ræskḷ]
名 調皮鬼，小淘氣

*cannot help ...*
沒辦法不⋯

**T**hey are very sweet but are little **rascals**. They **cannot help** getting into trouble.

他ㄊㄚ們ㄇㄣ很ㄏㄣ討ㄊㄠ人ㄖㄣ喜ㄒㄧ愛ㄞ，卻ㄑㄩㄝ也ㄧㄝ是ㄕ小ㄒㄧㄠ調ㄊㄧㄠ皮ㄆㄧ鬼ㄍㄨㄟ。他ㄊㄚ們ㄇㄣ沒ㄇㄟ法ㄈㄚ兒ㄦ不ㄅㄨ惹ㄖㄜ麻ㄇㄚ煩ㄈㄢ呢ㄋㄜ！

3

*mouse* [maʊs]
名 老鼠（單數）

*bake* [bek]
動 烘烤

*dip* [dɪp]
動 把（手）伸進…

*mix* [mɪks]
名 混合物

**M**rs **Mouse** is **baking** a cake in the kitchen.
Snore **dips** a finger in the **mix**.

老鼠媽媽正在廚房裡做蛋糕。諾諾把一根手指
頭伸到麵糊裡面。

4

| | |
|---|---|
| *cry* [kraɪ]<br>動 大聲叫 | 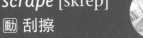 |
| *until* [ən`tɪl]<br>連 直到… | |
| *scrape* [skrep]<br>動 刮擦 | |
| *bowl* [bol]<br>名 碗，盆 | |

"**D**on't!" **cries** his mother. "Wait **until** I have finished. Then you can **scrape** the **bowl**."

「不行！」媽媽大叫著。「等我做好嘛！那時你們就可以把盆子舔乾淨了呀！」

**oven** [`ʌvən]
名 烤爐

**let** [lɛt]
動 讓

**M**rs Mouse puts the cake in the **oven**. Then she **lets** the twins have the bowl.

老鼠媽媽把蛋糕放進烤爐裡，然後把盆子給了嗳嗳和諾諾。

**S**omehow they **spread** cake mix all over their
**noses** and **whiskers** and the floor.

不知怎麼地，他們倆把鼻子、鬍鬚、整個地板弄得都是麵糊呢！

*scrub* [skrʌb]
動 擦洗

*shine* [ʃaɪn]
動 發光

rs Mouse **scrubs** the floor and the twins' faces until they **shine**. Then she says,

於是老鼠媽媽把地板和他們倆的臉蛋兒擦洗得閃閃發亮。然後她說：

"I need **cherries** for the cake. Can you go to Mr **Otter**'s **store** for me please."

「我需要櫻桃來做蛋糕。你們可以去水獺先生的店裡幫我買一些回來嗎？」

*scurry* [`skɝɪ]
動 匆忙地跑

 *scarecrow* [`skɛr͵kro]
名 稻草人

 *wave* [wev]
動 揮手

 *pass* [pæs]
動 經過

The twins **scurry** down Sunshine Hill. Mr Rags, the **scarecrow**, **waves** as they **pass**.

他們快步跑下陽光山丘。稻草人瑞格斯先生在他們經過的時候還揮了揮手。

*find* [faɪnd]
動 找到

*shelf* [ʃɛlf]
名 架子

**M**rs Otter **finds** some cherries on the **shelf**.
Snooze puts them in the basket.

水ㄕㄨㄟˇ獺ㄊㄚˇ太ㄊㄞˋ太ㄊㄞˋ在ㄗㄞˋ架ㄐㄧㄚˋ子ㄗ˙上ㄕㄤˋ找ㄓㄠˇ到ㄉㄠˋ一ㄧ些ㄒㄧㄝ櫻ㄧㄥ桃ㄊㄠˊ。嘮ㄋㄠˊ嘮ㄋㄠˊ把ㄅㄚˇ它ㄊㄚ們ㄇㄣ˙
放ㄈㄤˋ進ㄐㄧㄣˋ籃ㄌㄢˊ子ㄗ˙裡ㄌㄧˇ。

*rest* [rɛst]
名 休息

*half* [hæf]
形 一半的

It is hot walking back up the hill, and the twins sit down for a **rest half** way.

因为天氣很熱，在走回山丘的路上，他們倆就在半途坐下來休息。

**A** hungry **wasp flies** into the basket. He wants to **taste** the cherries in the **pot**.

這時，一隻飢餓的黃蜂飛進籃子裡面，他想要嚐嚐罐子裡的櫻桃呢！

13

*cap* [kæp]
名 帽子

"Go away," says Snore. "Those are not for you."
He waves his **cap** at the wasp.

「走ㄗㄡˇ開ㄎㄞ！」諾ㄋㄨㄛˋ諾ㄋㄨㄛˋ說ㄕㄨㄛ。「那ㄋㄚˋ不ㄅㄨˊ是ㄕˋ要ㄧㄠˋ給ㄍㄟˇ你ㄋㄧˇ的ㄉㄜˊ！」他ㄊㄚ揮ㄏㄨㄟ了ㄌㄜˊ揮ㄏㄨㄟ帽ㄇㄠˋ子ㄗˇ想ㄒㄧㄤˇ趕ㄍㄢˇ走ㄗㄡˇ那ㄋㄚˋ隻ㄓ黃ㄏㄨㄤˊ蜂ㄈㄥ。

14

*notice* [`notɪs]
名 注意

*shake* [ʃek]
動 搖動

*swing* [swɪŋ]
動 使旋轉

*around*
[ə`raʊnd]
副 兜著圈子地

The wasp takes no **notice**. Snore **shakes** the basket and then **swings** it **around**.

黃蜂可不理會呢！諾諾搖了搖籃子，接著把它拿起來轉了一圈。

**S**uddenly the basket, cherry pot, and wasp fly into the air and **land** on Mr Rags.

突然間，籃子、櫻桃罐和黃蜂全飛到空中去了，然後掉落在瑞格斯先生的身上。

16

*beam* [bim]
動 愉快地微笑

*cross* [krɔs]
形 發怒的

*buzz* [bʌz]
動 嗡嗡響

"Thanks! I need a new hat," says Mr Rags,
**beaming** as the **cross** wasp **buzzes** away.

「謝謝啊！我正需要一頂新帽子呢！」瑞格斯先生愉快地笑著說，而那隻生氣的黃蜂這時嗡嗡嗡地飛走了。

17

*explain*
[ɪk`splen]
勔 解釋

*delicious*
[dɪ`lɪʃəs]
形 美味的

*iced* [aɪst]
形 冰凍過的

"here is my basket?" Mrs Mouse asks. Snooze and Snore **explain** as they sit down to eat **delicious iced** cake.

「我ㄨㄛˇ的ㄉㄜ˙籃ㄌㄢˊ子ㄗ˙呢ㄋㄜ˙?」老ㄌㄠˇ鼠ㄕㄨˇ媽ㄇㄚ媽ㄇㄚ˙問ㄨㄣˋ。嗲ㄌㄠˊ嗲ㄌㄠˊ和ㄏㄜˊ諾ㄋㄨㄛˋ諾ㄋㄨㄛˋ一ㄧˋ邊ㄅㄧㄢ坐ㄗㄨㄛˋ下ㄒㄧㄚˋ來ㄌㄞˊ吃ㄔ著ㄓㄜ˙美ㄇㄟˇ味ㄨㄟˋ的ㄉㄜ˙冰ㄅㄧㄥ蛋ㄉㄢˋ糕ㄍㄠ,一ㄧˋ邊ㄅㄧㄢ解ㄐㄧㄝˇ釋ㄕˋ著ㄓㄜ˙。

*story* [`storɪ]
名 故事

*laugh* [læf]
動 笑

*bonnet* [`banɪt]
名 圓軟帽

"**W**hat a **story**!" **laughs** Mrs Mouse. "Well, I shall just have to ask for my basket back and give Mr Rags my old **bonnet**."

「真是個精彩的故事！」老鼠媽媽笑著說。「那好吧！我只需去要回我的籃子，舊圓帽就送給瑞格斯先生吧！」

19